THE MOUSE ON CAR #3

Written by Robin E. Kirk

Illustrated by Gail M. Nelson

STEUBEN PRESS
An Imprint of R&R Graphics Inc.

Copyright © TXu 1-597-425 November 1, 2007, Robin E. Kirk
Illustrations Copyright © 2009, Gail M. Nelson

Published and printed by:
    Steuben Press
    an Imprint of R&R Graphics, Inc.
    8547 E. Arapahoe Rd., J240
    Greenwood Village, CO 80112

Printed in the United States of America

Hardcover ISBN-13 978-1-935787-17-4
Paperback ISBN-13 978-1-935787-80-8

For friends, Ranger Pam and David who encouraged Maestro
to get 'on board!' and for my family, Mark, Ashley, Alan, and
Allie who helped to keep Maestro 'on track.'
REK

For my daughter, Katie, my niece, Delaney, and nephews: Ian,
Hayden, and Quin, who love *mousey stories*.
GMN

Hello, my name is Maestro (Micestro),
and I am a little brown mouse
who lives in a moving house.

I live on a train, specifically car #3,
and it's the best place a mouse could be.

Sometimes I sit on the top of the seats
to look through the windows.
The scenery is beautiful
winter, spring, summer, and fall.

Most of the time
I sit between the seats
hiding from one and all!

The train runs through the valley
in a national park.
It runs during the day
and sometimes at dark.

The Conductor, the train crew,
the engineer, too,
pass by my house
with many things to do.

Passengers come and go
through my car #3,
but never expect
to see a mouse like me.

So I stay quietly hidden
and listen and learn
about coyotes, deer,
beaver, and birds.

Coyotes howl and
yip at dusk.

Deer babies are called fawns.

Beavers build dams and lodge homes out of sticks and mud.

Cardinals are birds that eat seeds and fruit.

It's a big world out there
beyond my window seat,
but the things I see and hear inside
are always a treat.

Children on field trips with lunches in tow
leave delicious morsels
to munch on after they go.

Songs about birthdays, celebrations, and trains
add to the festivities along the way.

Stories are told about animals and people from the past.

I love to listen to the rangers in their flat hats.

Sometimes there is clapping, laughing,
singing, and dancing
on car #3!

What fun it can be!!

The train whistle blows
to warn those near the tracks:

Stay Back,
Stay Back,
Stay Back!

Clickety Clack,
Clickety Clack,
Clickety Clack!

The day is done.
Passengers had fun.

The crew say goodnight
and turn out the light.

I snuggle into my bed
between the seats.
Pleasant dreams for me on car #3.

ROBIN KIRK enjoys nature and children's stories. Robin lives in Ohio next to the beautiful Cuyahoga Valley National Park. She works and volunteers in the park and also on the Cuyahoga Valley Scenic Railway that rides through the park.

GAIL NELSON
loves to illustrate
books, draw,
paint watercolors,
and make
recycled paper.
She also enjoys
teaching cooking and gardening
camps and showing kids how to make
healthier choices.

To order copies of

THE MOUSE ON CAR #3

Hardcover ISBN 978-1-935787-17-4
Paperback ISBN 978-1-935787-80-8

You may order on line at:
www.SteubenPress.com

Order by phone at:
303-482-2060

STEUBEN PRESS
An Imprint of R&R Graphics Inc.